Garland Cove – Deborah Sheldon
Death In The Dugout – Bruce Harris

Beats! Ballads! Blank Verse!

Book 1: Echoes From An Expired Earth – Allen Ashley
Book 2: Grave Goods – Cardinal Cox
Book 3: From Long Ago – Paul Woodward
Book 4: Laws Of Discord – William Clunie
Book 5: Fanged Dandelion – Eric LaRocca

Weird! Wonderful! Other Worlds

Book 1: The Raven King – Liz Tuckwell
Book 2: The Wired City – Yolanda Sfetsos

Horror Novels & Novellas

House Of Wrax – Raven Dane
And Blood Did Fall – Chad A. Clark
The Fallen – Anthony Watson
The Underclass – Dan Weatherer
Cheslyn Myre – Dan Weatherer
Greenbeard – John Travis
Tower Of Raven – Kevin M. Folliard
Welcome Home Natalie – Reyna Young
Little Bird – TR Hitchman
Society Place – Andrew David Barker
Axe – Terry Grimwood
Wicked Blood – E.C. Hanson
The Again-Walkers – Deborah Sheldon
Between The Teeth Of Charon – Grant Longstaff

Science Fiction Novels & Novellas

Odyssey Of The Black Turtle – Paul Woodward
Sons Of Sol – Kevin R. McNally

The 'A QUIET APOCALYPSE' Series

A Quiet Apocalypse – Dave Jeffery

Cathedral (A Quiet Apocalypse Book 2) – Dave Jeffery

The Samaritan (A Quiet Apocalypse Book 3) – Dave Jeffery

Tribunal (A Quiet Apocalypse Book 4) – Dave Jeffery

A Silent Dystopia (Stories Of A Quiet Apocalypse) – Edited by D.T. Griffith

General Fiction

Joe – Terry Grimwood

Finding Jericho – Dave Jeffery

Science Fiction Collections

Vistas – Chris Kelso

Horror Fiction Collections

Distant Frequencies – Frank Duffy

Where We Live – Tim Cooke

Night Voices – Paul Edwards & Frank Duffy

Anthologies

The Darkest Battlefield – Tales Of WW1/Horror

DEMAIN PUBLISHING

Short Sharp Shocks!

Book 0: Dirty Paws - Dean M. Drinkel
Book 1: Patient K - Barbie Wilde
Book 2: The Stranger & The Ribbon – Tim Dry
Book 3: Asylum Of Shadows – Stephanie Ellis
Book 4: Monster Beach – Ritchie Valentine Smith
Book 5: Beasties & Other Stories – Martin Richmond
Book 6: Every Moon Atrocious – Emile-Louis Tomas Jouvet
Book 7: A Monster Met – Liz Tuckwell
Book 8: The Intruders & Other Stories – Jason D. Brawn
Book 9: The Other – David Youngquist
Book 10: Symphony Of Blood – Leah Crowley
Book 11: Shattered – Anthony Watson
Book 12: The Devil's Portion – Benedict J. Jones
Book 13: Cinders Of A Blind Man Who Could See – Kev Harrison
Book 14: Dulce Et Decorum Est – Dan Howarth
Book 15: Blood, Bears & Dolls – Allison Weir
Book 16: The Forest Is Hungry – Chris Stanley
Book 17: The Town That Feared Dusk – Calvin Demmer
Book 18: Night Of The Rider – Alyson Faye
Book 19: Isidora's Pawn – Erik Hofstatter
Book 20: Plain – D.T. Griffith
Book 21: Supermassive Black Mass – Matthew Davis
Book 22: Whispers Of The Sea (& Other Stories) – L. R. Bonehill
Book 23: Magic – Eric Nash
Book 24: The Plague – R.J. Meldrum
Book 25: Candy Corn – Kevin M. Folliard
Book 26: The Elixir – Lee Allen Howard
Book 27: Breaking The Habit – Yolanda Sfetsos
Book 28: Forfeit Tissue – C. C. Adams

Book 29: Crown Of Thorns – Trevor Kennedy
Book 30: The Encampment / Blood Memory – Zachary Ashford
Book 31: Dreams Of Lake Drukka / Exhumation – Mike Thorn
Book 32: Apples / Snail Trails – Russell Smeaton
Book 33: An Invitation To Darkness – Hailey Piper
Book 34: The Necessary Evils & Sick Girl – Dan Weatherer
Book 35: The Couvade – Joe Koch
Book 36: The Camp Creeper & Other Stories – Dave Jeffery
Book 37: Flaying Sins – Ian Woodhead
Book 38: Hearts & Bones – Theresa Derwin
Book 39: The Unbeliever & The Intruder – Morgan K. Tanner
Book 40: The Coffin Walk – Richard Farren Barber
Book 41: The Straitjacket In The Woods – Kitty R. Kane
Book 42: Heart Of Stone – M. Brandon Robbins
Book 43: Bits – R.A. Busby
Book 44: Last Meal In Osaka & Other Stories – Gary Buller
Book 45: The One That Knows No Fear – Steve Stred
Book 46: The Birthday Girl & Other Stories – Christopher Beck
Book 47: Crowded House & Other Stories - S.J. Budd
Book 48: Hand To Mouth – Deborah Sheldon
Book 49: Moonlight Gunshot Mallet Flame / A Little Death – Alicia Hilton
Book 50: Dark Corners - David Charlesworth

Murder! Mystery! Mayhem!

Maggie Of My Heart – Alyson Faye
The Funeral Birds – Paula R.C. Readman
Cursed – Paul M. Feeney
The Bone Factory – Yolanda Sfetsos

THE AGAIN-WALKERS

BY
DEBORAH SHELDON

The Again-Walkers was first published in *Perfect Little Stitches and Other Stories* by Deborah Sheldon (IFWG Publishing Australia, 2017)

For further information, please visit:
WEB: www.demainpublishing.com
TWITTER: @DemainPubUk
FACEBOOK: Demain Publishing
INSTAGRAM: demainpublishing

For Allen and Harry

CONTENTS

CHAPTER ONE

As she now must do every weekday morning, Svana left the house carrying the lunch-pail of bread, cheese and beer. The trek to the village centre was several miles. She walked faster than usual, a little breathless. The spring air was cool. A layer of snow still covered the peaks of the faraway ranges. She should have worn a shawl. Then again, she had planned all along to bare her shoulders and neck, regardless of the weather. Before leaving the house, she had laced her belt tightly to show off her narrow waist, had taken great care with her braiding so that an intricate criss-crossing of plaits encircled a cascade of yellow hair from her crown. Her mother-in-law, Dagny, had noticed. Looking up from the loom, the old woman had skewed an eye and said, "Don't be thinking about making mischief. Hallkell won't stand for it."

Humming, Svana patted at her hair with one hand, and swung the lunch-pail in the other. The lane began to widen and fill with foot traffic and people drawing carts behind horses or riding on horseback. No one waved or spoke to her. As a peace-pledge wife given by her father to appease Hallkell's family, Svana had resided here for about a month. Whether the villagers didn't talk to her because she was a foreigner, or because they were fearful of Hallkell's wrath, Svana didn't know. She had fled that first night, barefoot and crying, in the direction of her own village, but Hallkell had caught her and beat her. Neighbours had seen. They saw everything. No doubt, everyone in the village knew about Svana and Hallkell's wedding night.

Over the rise, the wooden buildings with their steeply pitched roofs came into view. Svana headed to the marketplace. A bustle of women, men, and children thronged the stalls. Dogs roamed. Hawkers called out to attract customers. Someone played a pan-pipe, the notes rising and falling. Svana headed to the foundry.

A great heat came from the furnace. She stood at Hallkell's side until he noticed her. He dismissed his apprentice, who left the foundry to purchase something to eat from the market. Putting down his tools, Hallkell strode away from the anvil and bellows, and took off his leather apron and gloves.

As was his custom, he didn't speak to her.

She handed him the lunch-pail. He sat on a bench and started eating. Hallkell was a giant of a man, fat and heavily muscled. He wore his dark blonde hair shaved apart from a single braid that followed the midline of his scalp to his neck and then dangled down his back in a long plait. He had a moustache and kept his beard in a half-dozen plaits. As he ate and drank, Svana regarded his grimy, sweat-stained body, his pot belly, and the whorls of hair matting his meaty shoulders. She curled her lip at the memory of his lovemaking. Just last night, he had lain on top of her, at arm's length, pumping mindlessly, staring at the wall. When she had tried to touch herself, he had slapped away her hands, saying, "Be still. You're a wife, not a whore." From the other bedroom behind a curtain, his mother, Dagny, had laughed.

Now, Hallkell belched and dropped the empty beer bottle into the lunch-pail.

"I need money," Svana said.

"For what?"

"Dagny has asked for skeins of wool."

Hallkell stood and searched through the leather money-pouch on his belt. He brought out some coins, and then a few more.

"Here," he said. "Buy yourself a piece of jewellery."

"I have enough jewellery already. Thank you, Husband."

"Then buy yourself a new dress." He gazed down at her and briefly touched her cheek. "You look pretty," he said.

"I try my best to please you."

"And you please me greatly. Now, be on your way."

He turned from her and picked up his leather apron. Svana pocketed the coins and moved through the marketplace. Hallkell had taken longer than usual over his lunch. It was past midday. Already, the meat, fruit and vegetable vendors were packing up and preparing to return to their farms. Was Svana too late? She hurried, slipping through the crowd, the pulse beating in her throat.

Relieved, she stopped.

Behind a trestle table arrayed with cuts of lamb and mutton was the shepherd, Agmundr, attending to a customer. Unlike the other villagers who had red, brown or blonde hair, Agmundr's hair was jet-black. He wore it parted on the side and long to his collar. Unusually, he was clean-shaven. Svana had never before touched the face of a clean-shaven man, and wondered how such a jaw-line might feel. Agmundr wasn't wearing his cloak today. Bare-armed in his tunic, the lean muscle and sinew moved beneath his pale skin as he wrapped the mutton for his customer. There was an exchange of goods and money. The customer spoke a few words and left. Agmundr looked across and saw her.

Caught, Svana held her breath.

The intensity of his gaze made her blush, clutch the lunch-pail in both hands.

She had first seen him three weeks ago at the Grand Hall assembly. The Earl and Wife had been recounting business affairs, conducting criminal trials and providing news of the outside world. As they did so, Svana had kept her chin in her hand, stifling yawns, when across the longhouse, she noticed a man watching her. His dark, heavily lashed eyes didn't look away. Jolted, Svana sat up. He smiled with one side of his mouth, his lips full and red. That night, she nudged at Hallkell for his sexual favour and imagined that she was making love with the mysterious, dark-haired stranger. By the next assembly in the Grand Hall, she knew the stranger's name and occupation: Agmundr Rask, shepherd. There was a dance to celebrate the start of spring, a line dance, men on one side and women on the other, so that everyone ultimately shared a turn. By the time she landed in Agmundr's arms, she was wet with anticipation. He held her close against his tensile body and seemed to stare into her very soul as he swung her around and around. She lost her breath, her gasp hidden in the tumult of music. Then, the next man took hold of her and Agmundr was gone. They kept catching each other's eye as the music played on and on, his mouth lifting at one corner, his eyes never blinking as if he couldn't afford to miss a second of her.

Over the past weeks, she'd lived for these glimpses, these stolen moments.

Now, she reddened as she walked past his stall.

Agmundr called out, "Is there something you want? Anything you need?"

Halting, she looked at him. With a wry smile, he spread both arms to encompass the meat on the trestle table. Then he raised his brows and gestured towards himself. Svana giggled. He laughed too. A lock of black hair fell across his brow. She wanted to smooth it back, wind her arms about his neck, and taste his mouth. A woman stopped and studied her, frowning. Chastened, Svana scurried past, almost breaking into a run. Hallkell's beating had been so terrible. It had taken her days to recover. Could she risk it again?

Agmundr, Agmundr...

Is there something you want? Anything you need?

Yes, she went ahead and bought Dagny's stupid skeins of wool, fussed over a variety of dresses and finally chose an expensive linen tunic, one that would befit the wife of a blacksmith, yet her mind lay elsewhere. By now, the market lane was almost empty of farmers. Svana could go straight home...or not.

Tradesmen like Hallkell would not finish work until dusk. She fidgeted at her complicated braids, ran a hand along the silky and golden hair that fell from her crown; touched the belt cinching her waist.

Then she walked north instead of east.

Agmundr's farm was a small, grassy plot with a thatched cottage at one end. Svana hesitated at the gate. Hurriedly, before she could change her mind, she entered the property and headed to the house. Sheep lifted their long, dull faces from the grass and watched her progress. Lambs broke away, kicking their heels and bleating.

The door was open. She stood within its frame.

Agmundr, sitting at the table with bread and cheese, stood up and swept the plates aside. He was wearing only trousers. His chest was wide and deeply split down the middle, his belly a cross-hatching of muscle. Svana's mouth went dry. She swapped the lunch-pail with its skeins of wool and its folded dress from one hand to the other. She'd prepared a speech before leaving home, had known all along what to say at this very moment, but the vision of a half-stripped Agmundr and those blue veins running along his forearms blasted her mind clean and empty.

"What are you doing here?" Agmundr said.

Svana fumbled with the money in her pocket. "I want lamb."

He smiled knowingly. Of course, she would have bought lamb at the market if needed. He gestured for her to come inside. Timidly, she stepped over the threshold. He took a wrapped piece of meat from a nearby bench and held it out. She took it and placed it in the lunch-pail. Numbly, she dropped uncounted coins onto the table.

"You are Hallkell's new bride," Agmundr said.

"Yes. My name is Svana Norup."

"You're a peace-pledge from another village?"

"My brother killed Hallkell's father. I'm the apology to stop the blood feud."

Agmundr moved out from behind the table. Svana's heart thrummed. Taking a step back, she remembered her suspicious mother-in-law, Dagny; the woman scrutinising her at the market; the various people who may have seen her walking to Agmundr's farm. She lost her nerve.

"I have to go," she said, and turned away.

"Wait."

He was behind her already, his hands gripping her arms. The air left Svana in a rush. Agmundr gathered her fall of hair and swept it aside to expose the nape of her neck. His touch brushed over her bare upper back, leaving trails that tingled and burned. Then he slipped his fingertips beneath the cowl of her dress and slid the fabric off one shoulder. His lips moved along her skin. The lick of his tongue on its way to the base of her neck made her shudder as surely as if his mouth had been nestled between her thighs. She leaned back into him. He clutched her waist and spun her around. His kiss was long and deep. As he drew up the folds of her dress, Svana quailed, and pushed him away.

"What's wrong?" Agmundr said.

"I can't. He'll kill me."

She kissed Agmundr passionately, desperately, for it would be the last time. Breaking away, she raced from the house.

"Come back," Agmundr called.

She kept running. The long road kicked up dust with every footfall.

Close to Hallkell's house, panting, feverishly wild and intoxicated, Svana ducked behind a stand of trees and hoisted up her dress. Rubbing at herself, she imagined Agmundr doing the same and fantasised the look on his face at the moment of release. She came, hard, and wiped her fingers on the grass.

Knees shaking, she took to the lane again. The sight of the thatched house brought tears to her eyes. Dagny would be waiting.

***

Dagny's loom clicked and clattered. Ignoring the headache that clenched her temples, Svana stirred the pot. Dusk had fallen. Birds called goodnight in the fading light. Hallkell pushed open the door and strode in, stinking of sweat and ash.

"What's for dinner?" he said. "It better not be rabbit."

Svana didn't look up from the pot. "Lamb stew."

"Lamb from whose farm?"

She said nothing.

Hallkell approached. "Agmundr's? I told you to stay away."

"I was with him only a few minutes."

Dagny stood up from her loom and clucked. "That's all it takes."

Svana smiled rigidly at her husband as he glared at her. "You must be tired," she said. "I'll fetch you a beer."

Hallkell grabbed her wrist.

"You're hurting me," she said.

"I don't like how that shepherd looks at you."

"He looks at me with both eyes, like everybody else. Let me go. Do you want the stew to burn?"

"I'm no fool. Agmundr eats you with his eyes. I've seen him at it."

Dagny shouted, "And Svana laps it up. I'll bet she's as wet as porridge."

Hallkell went to grope between Svana's legs, but she kept them clamped.

He cried, "Woman, what shame are you hiding?"

"None," she said, trying to twist free. "I'm your wife, I do you no harm."

"I provide and this is how you repay me? By running after a shepherd?"

The force of Hallkell's slap knocked Svana off her feet and headlong into the hearth. Before the flames could touch her, however, Hallkell dragged her clear by her hair. He gripped the golden hank that Agmundr had smoothed aside in order to press his lips against the nape of her neck. Dagny laughed and clapped at the drama.

"Are you all right?" Hallkell said, grasping Svana's shoulders and shaking her with all the strength in his prodigious arms, so that the teeth rattled in her head. "Did the fire touch you? By the love of Odin, are you all right? Tell me."

"Yes," she stammered. "I'm all right."

He shoved her and she fell against the table, panting. Only one thing in the world appeared to frighten Hallkell: fire. As a blacksmith, his body was covered in shiny red welts, and scars from countless burns. At that moment, if she could, Svana would have tied him to a stake and lit a huge pyre beneath him.

"Next time, answer me when I speak to you."

"Yes, Husband."

"Do not provoke me."

"Yes, Husband."

"Look at her hair," Dagny said, sidling over to stand by her son. "Do you see how much time and care she put into it today?"

Hallkell's face darkened. He looked at Svana from top to bottom, scrutinising her. She blushed. Hallkell must have seen the guilt in her face, for his chest started to rise and fall rapidly, and his hands clenched. It was as if Agmundr's kisses and fingerprints shone on her skin.

"Dagny," she said, and fell to the old woman's feet, clutching at her dress. "It wasn't I who killed your husband. Help me. Take pity on me."

Dagny sniffed, and pulled her skirts free. She resumed her seat at the loom.

Feeling cold and faint, Svana stood up. Hallkell advanced. On impulse, she plucked the carving knife from the table and held it out. He seemed surprised, even amused. When he began to shake his head at her, as if she had made a grave mistake, Svana felt the tears come. He stepped closer, a giant, an ogre, built so large he could enclose her neck in one hand. Trembling, she put down the knife.

"Please," she whispered. "Please don't."

"Woman, you give me no choice."

The beating took only a minute. He paused midway to chastise her.

"Quit mewling," he said. "It gets on my nerves. I spank you as lightly as I would a child. Why, if I hit you square just once, I'd dash your brains out. You ought to thank Odin for my mercy."

When he finished the beating, he told her to serve dinner. She obeyed. The thought of eating turned her stomach, but Hallkell wouldn't excuse her from the table. He and Dagny chatted about the events of the day. After the meal, Svana cleaned up. Then she went outside and sat by the water barrel, washcloth in hand. She kept dipping it in the water, wringing it out and holding it against her eye as a compress.

The distant mountains looked black against the sky. The first stars had started to shine. Far away, a pack of wolves yipped and called. Svana looked down at her wedding ring, forged by Hallkell and inscribed with tiny runes. He wore a matching ring. During the ceremony, they had offered these rings to each other on the hilt of Hallkell's new sword, made especially for the ceremony, as was the Viking custom. The Earl, who officiated, had spoken of the sword as a symbol: that the sanctity of their marriage vows could be broken only by death. The ceremonial sword hung on the kitchen wall. Svana had often dreamed of taking the weapon and using it to cleave Hallkell's neck in his sleep. But what fresh vengeance would his family then wreak against her own? Svana thought of her little sisters, her mother and grandparents, and wept.

The door opened.

Panicked, Svana straightened up and stopped crying. But it was only Dagny.

"Where is Hallkell?" Svana said, watching the doorway behind.

"Washing himself." Dagny seemed to consider for a moment. Then she closed the door, sat next to Svana on the bench, and patted her shoulder. This small gesture brought fresh tears.

"Don't blubber," Dagny said. "You know Hallkell can't bear the sound of it."

Svana dabbed at her eyes with the wet washcloth. "It's not fair. My brother murdered your husband, yet walks free. Why must I take my brother's punishment?"

"Because, as a woman, you're no better than a horse or an ox, a possession fit to barter. Your father should have taught you that lesson from birth."

Svana's throat ached with the need to cry. She dipped the washcloth, squeezed it, and held it to her eye. "I should be free to choose my own destiny."

"Hah. Do you have a cock? No, a defenceless slit. The world belongs to men." Dagny offered a weary smile. "Never mind all that. You must learn how to be Hallkell's wife, and learn quickly. Otherwise, one day you will enrage him enough to kill you." She sniffed and looked away. "I don't want my son to suffer punishment because of you."

"He treats me like a dog." The tightness in Svana's chest made her choke on her words. "I hate him."

Dagny knocked the washcloth from Svana's hand and rose. "Return to your chores," she said. "And if you have any sense, mind your husband. Stop giving him reasons to beat you."

While Dagny sat at the loom, Svana spent the rest of the evening kneading and baking loaves of bread, hanging milk curds in muslin cloth over a bucket, salting wheels of cheese, sorting the clothes for tomorrow's wash. The whole time, Hallkell drank beer. Svana kept count of the number of bottles. Four, five, six...his broad face became ruddy. He began to watch her carefully.

Then he stood, took his last drink, and said, "Woman, come to bed."

"I must unbraid my hair."

"Do it later."

He strode from the table and shoved through the curtain to their bedroom. Svana hesitated. Dagny made a clucking sound to catch her attention, and then gave an impatient gesture, urging Svana to follow him. Svana braced herself. It felt like walking to the gallows. She went through the curtains. Hallkell was lying in bed, already naked and erect.

"Take off your clothes," he said.

She fumbled with the brooches that pinned the straps of her woollen overdress. The overdress dropped to the floor. Then she pulled the cowled, ankle-length shift over her head and cast it aside. Hallkell smiled tenderly.

"You're very beautiful," he said. "I'm proud to have you as my wife."

She lowered her face and gazed at the dirt floor.

"Come," he said. "Lie on your back."

She did as she was told. He opened her thighs and knelt there. He spat between her legs and, cock in hand, began to work it inside her. She winced.

He made an exasperated sound. "Relax. You're too tight."

"I'm trying." Svana put an arm across her face. "You've blackened my eye. I'll not go to the General Assembly tomorrow."

"You'll go. Everyone in the village needs to see how Hallkell Jenson disciplines his wife." Grunting, he gave a final push. "There. Now be quiet while I attend to my business."

CHAPTER TWO

The following morning, they travelled to the village centre in the horse-drawn cart. Dagny sat up front, with Hallkell on the reins. Svana had to sit in the back. Despite her efforts with the cold washcloth, her eye was swollen and purple. Hallkell didn't appear to notice. He insisted that she wear her new linen dress to the General Assembly, her best necklace, and twist all of her hair into an intricate mesh of braids that sat like a crown on top of her head.

During the journey, Hallkell and Dagny kept waving and chatting to their neighbours who travelled the lane beside them on foot or horseback. Svana hardly dared look up. Any time she did meet someone's gaze, she saw pity or disgust.

What might Agmundr think of her now?

Outside the Grand Hall, the villagers gathered in groups to talk and laugh. Svana stood by Hallkell's side and stared at her boots. When the attendants opened the doors, Hallkell took her hand. Everyone filed inside. The Earl and Wife, richly dressed, sat high on a dais, their enormous chairs lined with furs. As usual, musicians played while everyone took their seats. Once the murmuring, shuffling of feet and coughing had stopped, the music stopped too. A horn sounded. The Earl began to talk of business, about a planned raid in another land far to the west. Svana didn't care. All she cared about was the humiliation of her swollen, purple eye. Next to her, she could hear Hallkell's nose whistling on each breath. Heat emanated from him like a fire, and he smelled sour and musky. Svana dug her fingernails into the wooden bench.

The Earl was a great orator. Villagers sat forward in their seats. Hallkell and Dagny were similarly transfixed. Keeping her head still, so as to not attract her husband's notice, Svana cut her gaze across the Great Hall. The sight of Agmundr clenched her insides. But Agmundr wasn't looking at her. No, he was glaring at Hallkell with a dark and murderous rage.

Svana could have wept in elation. There was a way out.

Agmundr loved her.

Now, by the gods, she had a way out.

***

The bruising subsided very slowly. Obsessed, impatient, checking her eye constantly in the mirror, Svana waited five days to see Agmundr. She hurried to the marketplace, gave Hallkell his lunch-pail as usual, watched him eat and drink. Then she stalked back and forth along the stalls. Kerchiefs, shoes, cloak-pins, caps, she cared for nothing of it. She watched the movement of the sun and waited. Whenever she passed Agmundr's stall, he stared at her and she looked back at him, brazenly. On each pass, the lust in his eyes made her loins shiver.

At last, the fresh food vendors packed up.

Svana waited a little longer, fussing over knitted socks. Finally, she bought two pairs: one for Hallkell and one for Dagny. She walked past Agmundr's empty trestle table. Steeling her resolve, she headed to his farm.

But he wasn't in his cottage.

Frozen at the doorway, Svana didn't know what to do. Perhaps he was consulting with a shearer or a wool-spinner. Disappointment hit her stomach. She ought to return to Hallkell's house, tend to the chickens, sweep the dirt floor; stop this fanciful nonsense.

"Svana Norup."

She turned. Agmundr stood with his bloody hands held out. She recoiled.

"Have no fear," he said. "One of my ewes gave birth. Give me a minute."

He shucked his stained shirt, scooped water from the barrel by the doorway and sluiced it over his head and body, washing himself. The water ran off him. Wet and shining, his brawn flexed and bunched. Svana, captivated, let go of the lunch-pail. It clattered at her feet. Agmundr shook his head. The droplets flew from his black hair. Smiling, he slicked back his fringe with one hand. His laugh brought out the muscles on his belly in sharp relief. Was he tormenting her, taunting her?

"What's so funny?" she said.

"I'm just glad to see you." He sobered. "I thought you'd never come back."

"If that were so, you could have visited me."

He raised his eyebrows. "And take on Hallkell Jenson?"

Svana picked up the lunch-pail in both hands. "So, you're afraid of him."

"Any man with a grain of sense is afraid of Hallkell Jenson."

She turned away to leave. Walking through the grass, she focused on the gate and its wooden slats. Sheep moved aside. Her feet felt heavy.

"What if I killed him?" Agmundr said from behind. He had followed her, soundlessly. "What then?"

Svana looked back. "You're too timid for such a deed. I can't afford the risk."

Agmundr gripped her arm and dragged her against him.

"Leave me be," she said. "This fate is my own."

"No. It's our fate together. The gods have decided. I have decided."

She gazed into his dark, sombre eyes.

"What if you did find the courage to murder Hallkell?" she said. "What if he rises after death, seeking vengeance? What then?"

Agmundr ran his hand through her hair. "Then I'll strike him down a second time and cut off his head."

"You're not frightened of an Again-Walker?"

"If it meant that I could take you as mine, I'd slay Hallkell a dozen times over, whether he were alive or dead."

"You would do that for me?" she whispered.

He brushed his lips over hers. "I would do anything for you."

His voice and touch dissolved her common sense. Svana allowed him to lead her behind the cottage, permitted him to pull her onto the green, soft grass. Agmundr lifted her dress and removed it. His mouth found her nipples. She arched her back against his lips. He kissed down, down, down along her stomach. Spreading her with his fingers, he lapped between her thighs. She worked her hands through his hair as the sensations arced sweet and sharp, higher and higher, tipping her over the edge. She cried out to the sky.

Recovering, gasping, she murmured, "You're all I've ever wanted."

Agmundr moved up her body and kissed her. She tasted her own juices. He unbuttoned and removed his trousers. Svana reached down and gripped him. He was large and thick; to her surprise, much bigger than Hallkell. Agmundr slid into her. Svana clasped at his hips and buttocks. Instead of pumping, he stayed deep inside and rocked against her, rhythmically, over and over; flooding her with pleasure, the sensations rising up and up and up as she strained against him.

"Oh, Agmundr," she sighed, and gritted her teeth.

The climax rolled through her, the intensity tricking her mind. The ground beneath her disappeared. She wrapped her arms and legs about him, frightened and exhilarated, clutching desperately as if the act of letting go would drop her through empty air, as if Agmundr suspended her above a precipice.

He moved to a kneeling position and lifted her up so that she sat astride. They pressed against each other, skin on skin, kissing. He began to move faster. His breath hitched. Svana gripped his ears with both hands and, rapt, watched his face. He returned her gaze for as long as he could. At last, grimacing, his eyes squeezed shut and he let out a guttural moan.

Spent, the lovers collapsed to the ground, panting.

A couple of sheep wandered over, curious. Agmundr struck out with a leg to chase them away. Svana giggled. With a smile, Agmundr caressed an errant curl of hair away from her cheek. Love shone in his adoring gaze.

She didn't want the moment to end, but it was now or never.

"What about Hallkell?" she said.

Agmundr's smile drained away. "Divorce him. He beats you, doesn't he?"

"Not enough to break bones. And I'm a pledge-wife. I don't have any rights. The Earl would never allow it. The blood feud between our families would only continue." She grabbed his arm. "You told me you would kill Hallkell. Was that a lie?"

Frowning, Agmundr gazed at the sky. "I don't wish to hang."

"So, make it look like an accident. Don't you want me for yourself?"

"I would be mad if I didn't."

Then he lay on his back with his arms behind his head and bit at his lips, deep in thought. Svana waited.

Finally, Agmundr turned his face to her. "Tomorrow is Sunday. Get Hallkell to visit me here at my farm. Now this is important: make sure he arrives on horseback. If he arrives on foot, my plan won't work."

"Do you really mean it?"

His eyes were steely. "I swear to you, Svana Norup, that Hallkell Jenson will be dead by this time tomorrow."

Unshed tears blurred her vision. She clasped her hands together at her mouth and laughed with relief, excitement, and gratitude. Then she took Agmundr's wrist and placed his palm directly on her breast, moving it so as to raise her nipple. When he stiffened against her thigh, she mounted him. Within seconds of entering her, Agmundr hardened into a full erection. He began to thrust.

She kissed him and sat up, riding.

"Oh, Svana," he chuckled. "If you keep on like this, you'll be the death of me."

***

After dinner, once the sun had set, Svana gave Hallkell and Dagny their presents: a pair of socks each. Dagny nodded her approval. Hallkell put his giant arm about Svana's waist and puckered his lips against her forehead.

"You are a good wife," he said, and then held out the socks to admire them.

"And you are a good husband."

"See, my little one?" he said. "I told you on our wedding night that we'd forge a life together."

Dagny stood from the table. "I shall gather the eggs."

She patted Svana's hair on her way past. When Dagny closed the front door behind her, Svana took a bottle of beer from the shelf, opened it and placed it front of Hallkell. Despite her resolve, her heart beat hard and fast with terror.

"Husband, there is something we need to discuss."

"I'm listening."

"You were correct about the shepherd, Agmundr Rask."

Hallkell slitted his eyes, swallowed his mouthful of beer, and carefully placed the bottle onto the table. "Explain."

"When I was at the market today..." Her throat closed up.

"Tell me."

Panic fluttered inside her stomach. "While I was buying your socks, I walked past Agmundr's stall and he told me that...he told me..."

Hallkell slammed his fist to the table. Svana cringed and gave a tiny shriek.

Mouth twisting, Hallkell said, "He told you what?"

"He told me that he wanted to bed me."

Hallkell's face filled with a slow, quivering rage. Blood suffused his cheeks. His arms trembled. Then he leapt from the table, grabbed his coat, and shouted, "I'll wring his head from his shoulders."

Svana panicked. "Now? But wait, it's too dark to travel."

"My fury will light the way."

"But the horse might stumble."

"I'll run every mile."

Svana flung herself on him and put her arms about his neck. Hallkell turned to the doorway. She swung helplessly, her feet off the ground. Agmundr had instructed that the visit be tomorrow. Agmundr wouldn't be ready yet, the plan wouldn't work.

"No, stay and give me comfort," she cried.

Hallkell paused. "Meaning what?"

"I'm frightened and need your warmth."

"Warmth?"

"I need my husband's love."

She began to kiss frantically at his cheeks, his beard, his mouth. Hallkell's beefy hands gripped her buttocks. Svana did her best not to flinch. His face still dark with anger, he walked her through the curtain and threw her to the bed.

"Lift up your dress," he said.

"But you'll stay the whole night with me? And visit Agmundr tomorrow?"

Hallkell stripped his trousers. "First thing after breakfast."

She opened her legs. "And take the horse. Don't waste energy on walking. You must be strong when you reach his farm. You must be strong and beat him."

Hallkell knelt onto the bed, his cock in hand. "Oh yes, Wife, but I'll do more than beat him. I shall kill that scrawny, boy-faced bastard."

She looked away.

He spat between her thighs. She pressed an arm across her face.

***

Sunday morning brought low clouds and a cool, misting rain. The horse's hooves beat a steady rhythm against the hard-packed dirt of the lane. Svana pulled the hood tighter around her face. Sitting behind her on the horse, Hallkell put his mouth to her ear, and said, "Are you cold? You're shivering."

"I shiver with worry. Please, halt the horse, let me get down. I'll walk home."

"No. I want to see Agmundr Rask eat you with his eyes one last time."

"But if you kill him, you'll hang."

Hallkell gave a dismissive grunt. "The Earl will forgive a crime of passion."

"I don't wish to see you fight. The very thought of it knots my stomach."

"Ease your mind, Wife. I'll not suffer a single scratch. If it's the violence that bothers you, look away and plug your ears while I deal the fatal blows."

She couldn't stop shaking. The journey to the village and beyond, to the farmlands, seemed to take an age. When she saw the thatched roof of Agmundr's cottage in the distance, dread ran through her. Hallkell must have felt it, for he took one hand off the reins to wrap a reassuring arm about her.

"Hush, little one, all will be well," he said. "You'll see."

"Perhaps you could just warn him."

He laughed. "Warn him? No. I'll not be cuckolded. Agmundr's death will be a lesson for any man stupid enough to covet my wife."

They reached the gate. Hallkell drew up the horse and dismounted. Svana raked her gaze over the property. There was no sign of Agmundr. Had he heard their approach? Was he prepared? Hallkell took hold of Svana's waist and lifted her down. He gave her the reins. Opening the gate, he smiled at her, and entered.

Palms sweating, knees quaking, she followed with the horse. Once she and the animal had passed through the gate, she found she could go no further. Hallkell strode across the grass towards the cottage. Both of his fists were clenched. Oh Frey, Svana prayed, son of Njord and brother of Freya, bestow your protection upon Agmundr, the man I love, the man who is to set me free from bondage. Please, Frey, I beg you...

Hallkell kicked open the cottage door and stepped inside. Svana put a hand to her mouth. But within a moment, Hallkell exited again, and shrugged.

The cottage must be empty.

Facing the grassy field with its dozens of sheep, he yelled, "Shepherd! You wish to bed my wife, do you? Come out from hiding and accept your punishment." He gazed around the field, as if expecting Agmundr to appear out of the faraway trees.

A movement caught Svana's eye.

Peeking from behind the cottage, holding a long-bearded axe, stood Agmundr.

Svana blanched.

He lifted a forefinger to his mouth – *shh* – and raced out, light-footed, silent and swift as a cat, the handle of the axe lifted over his shoulder.

With a great swing, he hit the blunt side of the axe against the back of Hallkell's head. Svana recoiled at the sharp cracking sound. Hallkell staggered, and dropped to his knees. Svana tried to look away but terror held her fast. Agmundr drew back the axe and swung again. This time, the blunt side of the blade made a wet and splintering sound. Hallkell fell onto his face. A small, burbling fountain of blood and dark curds erupted from the hole in his skull.

Working quickly, Agmundr wiped the axe on the grass and returned it to his cottage. He came outside again and flipped over Hallkell so that the dead man faced the sky. To do so took all of Agmundr's strength. Then he hurried to Svana and snatched the horse's reins from her. He turned the animal and struck its hindquarters. Whinnying, the horse took off through the gate at a trot, heading down the lane towards Hallkell and Dagny's house. Dizzy, Svana watched it go.

Agmundr grabbed her arms.

"Listen to me," he said. "This is what happened: the horse shied at something in the grass. Hallkell got bucked off and smacked his head. Cradle him in your arms and cry like a good wife. I will run to the village for a doctor. As far as we are both concerned, Hallkell is simply injured, not dead. When the doctor says that he is dead, you and I will be shocked and saddened at the news. Do you understand?" When she didn't answer, he shook her a little. "Svana, did you hear me?"

She nodded. Agmundr kissed her hard on her mouth, and ran out of the gate.

Long after he had disappeared from view, she kept staring down the empty path. The misting rain flurried and eddied in the breeze. Sheep bleated. Her heart boomed. She waited for Hallkell's giant hand to drop to her neck, for him to spin her around and slap her senseless. When nothing happened, she turned.

Hallkell lay exactly where Agmundr had left him.

She approached. His chest didn't rise or fall. His half-open eyes didn't blink. His frowning brows didn't relax.

"Husband?" she whispered.

She wiped rain from her face. Her hand trembled. She knelt down. The cold, wet dirt soaked through her overdress and shift. The ground near the cottage was indeed stony. It would seem plausible to the doctor that Hallkell had broken his skull on a rock. Hesitantly, she touched Hallkell on the arm.

He didn't respond.

A puddle of blood surrounded his head like a halo.

As Agmundr had instructed, Svana tried to cradle him. Gore smeared her palms. In revulsion, she wiped her hands on the grass. She decided to lie on his chest and stroke at his beard. To the doctor, racing to the scene of the accident, her posture would seem terribly sad and poignant, wouldn't it? She decided that it would.

She put her cheek to Hallkell's chest and stroked at his beard plaits.

Instead of relief, however, fear began to crowd her mind. It was important to placate Hallkell, for his spirit was close by and listening. Thankfully, he hadn't seen Agmundr's attack, and couldn't possibly know what had happened.

"Husband," she said. "When in your grave, please, sleep quietly. Your death was an accident. You fell and hit your head. Blame no one. Don't seek vengeance. What is there to avenge? You smashed your own brains. As your wife, I swear it."

But she could feel the coiled tension pent up within his corpse. Hallkell Jenson was not the kind of man who would surrender willingly to death. Anger would fuel his reanimation; transform him into a living corpse, an Again-Walker. She knew this to be true as surely as she knew that the sun rises and sets each day.

She began to cry.

By the time Agmundr returned with the doctor, and various other villagers who wanted to bear witness, Svana was hysterical. Two men hauled her by both arms from Hallkell's body as she wailed in horror of what was to come. Assuming her to be grief-stricken, the women tried their best to hold and comfort her.

The men stood back, awkward and embarrassed. When the doctor pronounced Hallkell dead, Svana finally looked at Agmundr. He was staring back at her, white-faced, his black hair slicked down with rain and sweat.

CHAPTER THREE

Hallkell's three uncles were as big, meaty, bearded and blonde as Hallkell himself. With their own hands, they built Hallkell's barrow, a pit lined with stone and fitted with a timber roof, which they dug high on the cemetery's hillside so that Hallkell's spirit could watch over the village for eternity.

Then the uncles had come to the house to help Svana and Dagny prepare the body. Upon arrival, however, they had first taken their revenge and slaughtered the horse, which had bucked off Hallkell and killed him with a hoof to the head, according to the doctor. The horse's last scream sounded like that of a woman.

Now, rattled, Svana gazed down at Hallkell. She, Dagny and the uncles had washed him, dressed him in his best clothes, put him face-up on a stretcher along the marital bed. In his arms, they had placed his blacksmithing hammer, tongs and poker, a pair of tweezers, comb, and a frying pan. He seemed larger in death than in life.

"We should cremate him," Svana whispered.

Dagny recoiled. "Put him in fire? With him so afraid of it?"

"Don't blame the child," one of the uncles said. "She fears he'll become an Again-Walker. We fear the same. Hallkell's spirit won't rest easy in the ground."

Another uncle added, "The only sure way is to burn his corpse to ashes. What difference would it make? He'll still have his barrow, after all, and his belongings to see him through the afterlife whether he's burned or not."

The third uncle said, "No. There are more respectful methods we can use."

"None of them as good as cremation," Svana said.

"It's up to Dagny," the first uncle said. "She birthed him. What is your word?"

Dagny glared at them, each in turn, with her rheumy and wounded eyes. "All right," she said at last. "We'll take precautions. But we'll not cremate him, you hear?"

The uncles agreed. Svana, uneasy, said nothing.

They placed an open pair of scissors on his chest, and twisted lengths of straw into crosses, which they put beneath his shroud. They tied his big toes together and stuck the soles of his feet with many needles. When the uncles carried his stretcher from the house, they raised and lowered it a couple of times at the threshold to form the shape of a cross. While they placed him in the cart, and secured the cart to two of their horses, Svana and Dagny went around the kitchen and put all of the pots and pans upside-down, and turned over the chairs.

"Do you think that will be enough?" Svana said.

Dagny's eyes glittered with hatred. "I know it was you."

The blood left Svana's face.

"I don't know how, but it was you and that shepherd," Dagny hissed, and waggled a finger. "Sleep with one ear open. My son will come back for you."

Svana fled from the house. One of the uncles kindly helped her into the cart. For once, she sat in the front seat and felt great satisfaction. Dagny had to sit in the back with the two remaining uncles and Hallkell's corpse.

They travelled to the cemetery in silence.

The entire village turned out for Hallkell's burial.

The parson prayed for Hallkell with magical words meant to bind the giant to his barrow, yet Svana perspired. She allowed herself two glimpses of Agmundr. Both times, he was watching her. What if anyone else saw him staring like that? So blatantly, so hungrily? Svana put her face in her hands. One of Hallkell's uncles mistook her gesture for grief, and put his great arm about her shoulders. It felt like Hallkell's arm. It felt like an omen.

There was a funereal feast in the Great Hall. Speeches were given. Hallkell's apprentice, a young man with long red hair, was named as the new blacksmith. The whole time, Svana could feel two sets of eyes scalding her skin: those of Agmundr and of Dagny. She kept her gaze on the floor. She accepted the condolences of the villagers, one by one, without looking up. A few of the women, apparently moved by her stoicism, wept for her. "Look, Svana's broken heart is numb," she heard one cry.

Afterwards, drunk, one of the uncles took Svana and Dagny home in the cart. With a wave, he turned the horses around in the courtyard and headed back to the village at a trot. Now it was just Svana and her ex mother-in-law.

Once they lit the lamps, Svana said, "I'll wait one more week. Then I'll ask the Earl if my peace-pledge can be voided. If the Earl says yes, I'll return to my village. If he says no, I'll serve you until another man claims me as his wife."

"Either way," Dagny sneered, "you'll have Agmundr between your legs."

Svana offered a sly, smug grin.

Nostrils flaring, Dagny said, "Revolting child! Go and gather the eggs."

"Gather them yourself," Svana said, and went to bed. She couldn't sleep for frayed nerves, but nonetheless, it was gratifying to hear Dagny outside the windows, fussing and swearing around the chicken coop as the hens clucked and flapped.

Finally, when Dagny extinguished the lamps and retired, Svana turned over and closed her eyes. The smell of Hallkell rose from the linen. Her pulse skittered.

Husband, she thought, stay in your barrow. There's nothing for you here now.

It took a long time to calm herself. At last, exhausted, Svana fell asleep.

***

A continuous pounding at the door woke her. Svana rubbed her eyes and rolled off the bed. A faint light lay about the house. The pounding continued. Svana stumbled across the kitchen. Dagny flipped aside her bedroom curtain and, perplexed, scrubbed at her wrinkled face and wandered out, flat-footed.

Svana called, "Who is it?"

"One of the Earl's messengers," said a male voice. "All occupants within, come out directly. There's a cart outside for you."

"What's going on?"

"An emergency assembly at the Grand Hall."

Svana unlatched and opened the door. Dawn streamed inside the house. The messenger startled, appeared to recognise her, and looked her carefully up and down. Svana clutched the nightclothes about her throat. A premonitory chill ran through her.

"I'll not go anywhere until after breakfast," Dagny said.

"Get dressed, both of you," the messenger ordered. "We leave now."

***

The villagers in the Grand Hall clustered together in frightened groups. According to Dagny, the last time the Earl had called an emergency assembly was more than ten years ago, when a mysterious form of sleeping sickness had struck the cattle on a particular farm. Svana watched the front of the longhouse. While the Wife sat in her fur-lined chair, waiting, the Earl was off to one side of the dais, consulting with his messengers. When the messengers left the dais to stand guard at the doors, the Earl gestured to his musicians. One of them stood up, and blew a long note on the horn. The villagers scrambled to sit. A hush descended straight away. Nonetheless, the musician blew a short note on the horn to introduce the Earl, who took his seat next to his

Wife and patted her arm. Together, the Earl and Wife gazed about at the congregation, tension etched in their faces.

Svana twisted on the thorns of a terrible anticipation. She knew what this emergency assembly was about. She already knew in the pit of her stomach.

The Earl announced, "We have an Again-Walker."

A loud murmur ran through the assembly. Svana felt faint.

"And we believe it to be Hallkell Jenson," he added.

People exclaimed. A couple of women shrieked. Svana's heart jangled. The villagers turned this way and that, looking for her and spotting her, some pointing her out to others. She wiped clammy hands along her overdress, over and over.

A short note sounded on the horn. The place fell silent.

"This is what we know," the Earl said, and crooked a finger.

A small, bent old man stood up and, blushing, faced the assembly.

The Earl said, "For those of you who don't know him, this is Claus the goat farmer. His property backs onto the cemetery. A few hours after sunset, he awoke to the sounds of his animals screaming. He went outside with a lantern and axe, fearing a wolf. The goats were running at full speed around and around the perimeter of the fence, frothing at the mouth in terror. Chasing them was not a wolf, but a huge, black bull, its skin half-flayed to show the red meat beneath. Only a man such as Hallkell Jenson would be large enough to transform into a bull."

Shocked muttering broke out in the longhouse. Svana peeked at Dagny beside her. The old woman was rigid and shaking, grinding her teeth, staring at the Earl.

Raising his arms to quieten the crowd, the Earl continued, "Knowing this huge flayed bull to be an Again-Walker, Claus went inside and barricaded the door. The bull ran his flock ragged for hours. The Again-Walker shifted its shape, for then Claus heard the beast climb onto his roof and start drumming at it with two heels. Sometime after midnight, the Again-Walker left. Claus went outside to check on his stock. Eight of his goats had been ridden to their deaths."

Discreetly, the Earl gave a small, dismissive gesture and Claus returned to his seat. The Earl crooked his finger at someone else.

Agmundr stood.

Svana's heart seemed to cramp. Mouth open, she gaped at him. Agmundr's eyes searched the crowd, found her. They stared at each other in shared agony for a moment. He lowered his gaze.

The Earl said, "For those of you who don't know him, this is Agmundr the sheep farmer. His property backs onto Claus's property. In a similar fashion, Agmundr woke to the sounds of his animals in distress. When he went outside, he found a dozen of his sheep crushed to death. Of the Again-Walker, there was no sign."

The faint noise of crying took up in the longhouse. Young, frightened children were clutching at their mothers. Everyone looked ashen and pinched.

The Earl's Wife spoke up. "Until we can hire a warrior to hunt and kill the Again-Walker," she said, "we must take great care. Do not go to the cemetery at any time. Do not be outside after dark. If you can, keep your animals inside with you at night. If there comes a knocking at your door at night, especially if it is a single knock, do not open it. Keep an iron sword on hand. If the Again-Walker rides your house, hide in case it breaks the roof beams and gains access. Do not try to flee, or the Again-Walker will catch you and destroy you."

Moans and murmuring started up.

The Earl raised his hands for attention, but was ignored. Lifting his voice, he said over the tumult, "We must pray to the gods for guidance. We don't yet know what torment has led the departed Hallkell Jenson to become an Again-Walker."

Dagny stood and shouted. "I know exactly what torment!"

Everyone fell quiet.

The Earl and Wife looked too shocked to be offended at the interruption.

Dagny pointed at Agmundr, who still stood at the foot of the dais, and said, "All along, he had unclean notions about Hallkell's wife, Svana. Like a whore, she invited Agmundr's attentions. Together, they drove Hallkell mad with jealousy."

The Earl and Wife gazed speculatively at Agmundr. A hot, prickling dread broke out across Svana's body. Sweat popped on her upper lip.

"Is this true?" the Earl said.

"The poor old woman is torn up with grief," Agmundr said. "She's keen to blame someone, anyone, for her son's untimely death."

Dagny said, "On the day he was killed, Hallkell visited Agmundr's farm to punish him. At the market, Agmundr had told Svana of his intent to bed her."

The congregation gasped.

The Earl said, "Svana, where are you?"

When she didn't move, Dagny slapped at her. Reluctantly, Svana stood.

"Come up here to the front," the Earl said, "where we can see you better."

Dagny shoved her. Svana sidestepped along the benches to reach the aisle. Villagers pulled their knees out of her way, quickly, as if she might burn them with the merest brush of her dress. She approached the dais and stood there, hands clasped in front of her, skin flushed and hot.

The Wife said, "What have you to say about this?"

"Nothing, my Lady," Svana whispered.

"Nothing? Not a word in defence of your honour?"

"Ask anybody," Dagny shouted. "Agmundr is forever making cow-eyes at her."

"All right," the Earl said. "Any witnesses?"

Mortified, Svana looked about at the dozens of raised hands.

"So, a man admires a beautiful girl," the Wife said, and shrugged. "A cat may look at a Queen, after all, with no harm done. Plenty of men would ogle Svana. How could they not? She is young with soft yellow hair, big blue eyes, and skin like milk. Hallkell should have known better than to lose his senses over one of his wife's many secret admirers. Svana, Agmundr, you may both return to your seats."

The relief surging through Svana made her legs shake. She glanced at Agmundr. He smiled at her, faintly, with one side of his mouth. His dark eyes shone.

"Wait, my Lord and Lady," said a male voice.

Svana turned to see who had spoken. The blood ran to her feet. Standing up was Esbern, the chicken farmer, and his wife, Kirsten. They were next door to Agmundr's property. In fact, she had twice passed by their fence on her way to Agmundr's gate. The Earl raised one palm to Svana and Agmundr, as if to say, *stay there*, and crooked the forefinger of his other hand at Esbern and Kirsten.

The couple approached the dais.

Svana felt ill.

"Speak your piece," the Earl said.

The couple regarded each other. Finally, after clearing his throat, Esbern said, "We are Agmundr's neighbours. On Saturday, the day before Hallkell died, my wife and I were tending to our chores when we heard noises of love-making. We went to the fence we share with Agmundr. There, we saw him lying in the grass with Svana."

Pandemonium erupted. The Earl's messengers had to race through the longhouse and strike out with staffs to force people to take their seats. The musician kept tooting his horn. Svana regarded Agmundr. His face was grey and frightened. She wanted to drop to the flagstones.

Order was restored after a long minute.

The Earl frowned. "Neighbours, are you absolutely sure?"

"Yes," Kirsten said. "They were naked and kissing each other. We saw them make love in various positions. He even put his mouth on her womanhood."

Uproar ensued. It took the messengers and the horn-player a good couple of minutes to calm the assembly.

"They murdered my son," Dagny shouted. "Svana lured him to Agmundr's farm where they both killed him. Our horse would never shy. Our horse would never have kicked Hallkell."

"Doctor," the Earl said. "Could Hallkell's cause of death have been something other than a horse's hoof?"

The doctor stood and scratched his beard. "Well...yes, I suppose."

The Earl sat forward in his chair. "Agmundr Rask, Svana Norup, it is time to confess. As lovers, did you conspire together to murder Hallkell Jenson?"

Lightheaded, Svana looked at Agmundr. Neither spoke.

The Wife clapped at one of the messengers and said, "Fetch a poker."

The room began to whirl. Svana felt a tight grip on her arms. Two of the Earl's messengers were holding her upright. A third was advancing with a poker. Glowing red and smoking, the poker smelt like sulphur, like Hallkell after a day at the foundry.

"Interrogate the girl first," the Earl said.

"Stop!" Agmundr bellowed.

Everyone froze. The longhouse went quiet. Dazed, Svana looked at Agmundr. He was sweating freely, but kept his shoulders squared.

"Leave her be," he said. "And I'll confess."

The Earl nodded. The messenger wielding the poker stepped back.

"Project your voice so that all can hear," the Wife said.

"So be it." Agmundr faced the crowd and lifted his chin. "I fell for Svana Norup the first moment I saw her. She holds my heart even as I speak."

Svana went limp. The messengers held her firmly.

"I wanted her for myself," Agmundr continued. "I didn't care that she was married. On Saturday, the day my neighbours thought they saw us making love, I had lured Svana on false pretences. When she insisted on being faithful to her husband, I forced myself upon her. My neighbours heard her cries of pain, not passion."

The villagers reacted with hisses and angry clamour.

Svana's eyes stung with tears.

The Earl lifted a silencing hand. "So, you admit to rape," he said. "Go on."

"The next day, she brought Hallkell to punish me. I slew him with an axe."

Waiting until the excited chatter around the longhouse abated, the Earl's Wife said, "Svana, why didn't you come to us and report these crimes?"

Agmundr said, "Because I swore I would kill her if she did."

The crowd turned ugly. The men were half-standing, shaking their fists, while the woman snarled through their teeth and whistled. Svana caught Agmundr's eye. He nodded at her, solemnly, and tried to smile with one side of his quavering mouth.

The Earl announced, "We have the full confession of Agmundr Rask, rapist and murderer. The sentence is death, to be carried out immediately."

Two messengers grabbed Agmundr.

A tidal wave of people carried Svana out of the double-doors. Still held by her arms, she was marched to the courtyard behind the longhouse amongst a sea of furious villagers. They cheered and yelled. The sunlight dazzled her. She kept tripping over her own feet. The strong hands of the messengers kept hauling her up.

"Agmundr," she wailed, but her voice was lost in the hubbub.

She was tossed to and fro. The voices around her rose, fell, and screamed to a feverish pitch. She opened her eyes. High above her, standing on the wooden trapdoor of the gallows, stood Agmundr, his arms behind his back, the hangman already placing the noose about his neck. She and Agmundr gazed into each other's souls in terror and frantic longing.

"Have you any final words?" the hangman said.

"Yes," Agmundr said, his voice trembling with emotion. "Svana, I love you."

She couldn't bear to watch. She screwed her eyes shut. The trapdoor clanked and clunked as it dropped. She heard the whisk of his body through space, the snap of the rope, the kick of his legs, and then nothing but the baying crowd.

The world spun too fast on its axis. Svana lost consciousness.

CHAPTER FOUR

The rest of the day was spent at the Grand Hall, with animal sacrifices, feasting, music and dance to curry favour from the gods. Every villager tried to seem happy and confident, since tears and begging only peeve the gods and make them contrary. Svana, however, sat on a bench and stared at the floor. From time to time, people came by to press goblets of beer or plates of food into her indifferent hands. Well-meaning women came over to tell her that, while it was no consolation, at least her husband's murderer had been dispatched from this world. Svana never answered.

Eventually, the Earl's Wife approached.

"You're making everyone uneasy," she said. "Come with me." She led Svana to an ante-chamber at the rear of the dais, a dressing-room richly decorated in furs, silver and gold. "Rest here," she added, gesturing at a divan.

Dutifully, Svana sat. The Wife took hold of Svana's feet and swung her legs so that Svana found herself lying down.

"There, is it not comfortable? I recline here to listen while the Earl rehearses his speeches." The Wife sat alongside and stroked at Svana's hair. "Poor girl, your short time in our village has been so very traumatic. I will appeal to the Earl to void your peace-pledge. You can return home to your family as soon as you feel able."

Svana nodded.

"Try to sleep," the Wife said, and left the ante-chamber, closing the door.

The merry, jaunty music sounded through the wooden walls. Svana stared at the rafters. Agmundr, Agmundr... *Is there something you want? Anything you need?* Yes, she thought, I need you, the warmth of your arms and the love in your eyes. On the other side of the wall, villagers gave out forced laughs and desperate cheers.

When the afternoon waned into early evening, the celebrations broke up so that everyone could hurry home before dusk.

Svana trudged along the lane. Dagny insisted upon walking next to her. Svana didn't wish to speak, but Dagny fidgeted as if she were full of words, opening her mouth and shutting it again, tutting to herself, stamping with a heavy tread.

Finally, she said, "Witch, Hallkell will come for you."

"Yes," Svana sighed. "I expect he will try."

"Despite your lies, I know you conspired with Agmundr. I know you're as guilty as he is.

You should have been hanged too, and thrown away."

"Shut up, old woman."

Tears blurred Svana's vision. After Agmundr was flung onto the rubbish tip, all the villagers had filed past to spit on him, as was the custom for criminals. His blood had not yet settled, so he appeared alive and only sleeping. Svana had wanted to gather him against her breast. The messengers had shaken her, insisting that she spit. She had cried that her mouth was dry, but the messengers only relented once the fury and disgust of villagers had shamed them into walking her past the body.

Now, Dagny gave a laugh. "Hallkell will pop your head like a bilberry."

Svana said nothing.

"You hope I'll put in a good word?" Dagny went on. "Not a chance. I shall stand aside and let him have at you. I'll applaud Hallkell as he rends your limbs."

The air held a chill. Svana gathered the cloak tighter around her shoulders. Her silence, however, seemed only to provoke Dagny's suspicion.

"Why aren't you afraid?" the old woman said.

Because I no longer care if I live or die, Svana thought. But she didn't answer.

"Oh, I get it," Dagny said. "You imagine that love will transform Agmundr into an Again-Walker. You believe he'll protect you from Hallkell's wrath."

"I believe no such thing."

"Yes, you do. So young and stupid, hah, you know nothing of men."

Svana kept walking. In the distance, a pack of wolves yipped and bayed. The sky began to look bleached about its edges.

"A woman's love is selfless," Dagny continued. "She would die for her child, but a man can't fathom such a gesture. A man's love is fickle and self-centred. If you don't please him, and keep pleasing him, he will turn on you."

Not Agmundr, Svana thought grimly.

As if reading her mind, Dagny cackled. "That is the way of all men, your precious Agmundr included. He won't rise from death to help you. But he might rise to take vengeance upon you. After all, you're to blame for his hanging."

They reached the house. Svana chased the chickens into the coop and collected the eggs in the apron of her overdress. Momentarily, she considered bringing the animals inside the house, as the Earl's Wife had instructed, but upon reflection, she didn't care a jot if Hallkell, in his supernatural form, slew his own livestock. She decided to leave open the door of the coop. If Hallkell didn't kill the chickens, let the wolves have them. She cast her gaze across the land. The stars had started to glow in the deepening sky. No one in the village would sleep easy tonight. In fact, no one would sleep easy again until the Again-Walker was killed.

Svana came inside. Dagny, wielding a large knife, was slicing root vegetables into a pot of simmering water over the fire.

Svana put the eggs into the basket, and said, "Do you want help?"

"So that you can poison me?"

"You're a spiteful bitch. I hate you almost as much as I hated your son."

Svana stormed to the marital bedroom and glared about. She despised every piece of furnishing. Tomorrow, she would leave and never return. She began folding her clothes – tunics, overdresses, aprons, cloaks, hats, shoes – and placing them inside her two large leather bags. Hallkell had given her many items of jewellery over the weeks of their marriage. These items she placed inside a linen drawstring pouch. Once she was home in her own village, she would be safe. Again-Walkers could not trespass onto foreign soil. Hallkell's reanimated corpse would be stuck in this village until a warrior killed it and sent the restless spirit shrieking into the afterlife.

A corner of the bedroom curtain twitched aside.

"What do you think you're doing?" Dagny said.

"Packing."

Dagny opened the curtain. "To leave? On whose authority?"

"The Earl's Wife. She voided my peace-pledge. I'm going home tomorrow."

Dagny upended one of the bags and said, pointing, "Not with that or that or that. Hallkell bought those."

"And presented them to me as gifts."

Dagny tightened her lips. "Oh no, you won't take his gifts with you."

"And who is going to stop me?"

A single knock sounded at the door, impossibly loud, as if hammered not with a fist but with a tree trunk. The women froze. With the same wide-eyed expression, they waited for the visitor to knock again. The second knock didn't come. Svana's stomach clenched. The tendons along Dagny's stringy neck stood out in sharp relief. For a moment, the old woman appeared as scared as Svana, but a cruel smile lit up her face and made her eyes gleam.

"He has returned for you," she said. "Witch, it's time for your comeuppance."

She darted from the bedroom. Svana ran after her. Dagny was at the door.

"No," Svana yelled. "Don't open it."

Dagny threw the bolt. Lifting the latch and flinging aside the wooden door, she cried, "My son, my beloved son. Step inside and warm yourself. I shall bring you a beer. Slake your thirst, and then kill your stone-hearted viper of a wife."

Nothing happened for long moments.

The only sounds were the crackle of the fire, the bubbling of the stew, Dagny's excited puffing and panting. Svana stared at the doorway. It held total and utter blackness, as if a moonless night had somehow descended from the sky and wrapped its arms around itself, like a bat, and barricaded the single exit. The night moved. Svana saw that it was a humanoid figure, a titan. Dark as coal, it stooped to fit its head and shoulders beneath the lintel, and shuffled crabwise to squeeze its bulk through the opening. Standing to its full height, its head grazed the rafters.

Svana stopped breathing.

Dagny staggered back, clutching at her chest.

This thing was Hallkell, yes, but just barely. Svana recognised the single braid along the scalp, the pattern of beard plaits. Swollen to twice Hallkell's size, the bloated and blackened Again-Walker regarded them both with care, one at a time and curiously, as if it couldn't quite place them in its memory. The eyes were not human. They reflected the lamplight as would a pair of mirrors. The Again-Walker growled. Its breath stank, rotten and fetid, like the gas that rises from a swamp.

The four windows were small, designed to keep out the cold. The only one that might be large enough to allow egress was next to the fireplace.

"Step away," Svana said. "We can try to escape through the back window."

"Escape? Why should I, when I have nothing to fear?" Recovered from her initial fright, Dagny closed the door and drew the bolt, locking them all inside. Sneering, she hissed, "Look what you did to my boy. I shall laugh as he stamps you to death. Did you hear me? Laugh! And when he's done, I'll stamp on you too."

"That monster is no longer your son. It'll kill us both."

"Hah, watch this." Dagny spread her palms to the Again-Walker, and whispered, "Don't you know me, Hallkell? Your own dear mother, the one who brought you into this world and nursed you?"

The Again-Walker held out its enormous arms and cradled Dagny's head between its hands, tenderly, as if to draw her closer for a kiss. At first, Dagny smiled. Then, grunting, she began to struggle. She screamed. Blood ran from her ears. Her skull cracked as loudly as a nut. The Again-Walker released its grip. Dagny dropped to the floor, blood spraying in jets from her broken head.

Svana withdrew across the kitchen. The Again-Walker stared with a blank face. Its footsteps shook the walls. Svana backed against the fireplace.

Trapped...

No, perhaps she had a chance.

From the hearth, she drew a flaming log and held it out. In life, Hallkell had been afraid of fire. Surely, his Again-Walker would share the same dread?

"Retreat," she yelled, waving the log. "Retreat or I shall burn you."

The Again-Walker didn't seem to notice. Its metallic mirror-eyes reflected the fire. Svana lunged with the flaming log, close enough to singe the beard plaits. The hair shrivelled and released an acrid smoke. Keening, the Again-Walker balked.

Svana, gasping, tried to make sense of this.

Had the heat of the fire stirred what was left of Hallkell's memory?

Yes, that must be the explanation. What else could it be? Svana kept swinging the log. The monster kept backing up. She had to steer it away from the door. But no, too soon, the flames smouldered and went out. The Again-Walker regarded her with annoyance. And the fireplace lay too far away to grab another burning log.

She stared up into the monster's eyes. Reflected was her terrified face. The hands reached out to enclose her head. Ducking, Svana dropped the log. She ran to put the table between them. The table was too small to lead the Again-Walker on a merry chase, not big enough to allow her sufficient time to reach the door or climb through the window without being caught. Perhaps she could do laps of the table and grab one burning log after another, and scare the Again-Walker until sunrise when it must return to its barrow. But how long until the monster realised that all it need do was toss the table aside? Svana grabbed a carving knife from the table. Doubling over, she screamed from her diaphragm, ready to fight, ready to die.

"Damn you," she yelled. "You were never man enough to be my husband."

The monster paused, drew up a lip. The yellowed teeth were long and fanged.

"I despised being your wife," she said. "You were less than a pig."

The Again-Walker flinched as if stung. Svana lifted the knife. With its face twisting into a furious grimace, the Again-Walker began to suck air in and out of its mouth, as loudly as a pair of bellows, while it stood tall and taller still, ballooning higher and wider, its blistered skin splitting all over to reveal meat and a crawl of insects. Svana cowered. Soon, the Again-Walker was so big that it had to crouch beneath the ceiling. Now it would kill her.

A thundering noise began overhead.

Both Svana and the Again-Walker startled and looked up. Outside, on the roof, a noise like heels drummed, rattling the rafters. The drumming stopped. A section of thatching tore back. Svana stared into the patch of dingy sky. The knife shook in her fist. Could it be...?

Out of the darkness appeared a pale face framed by black hair.

Elated, Svana cried out, "Agmundr!"

He dropped from the roof and landed on the kitchen table.

She recoiled at his pungent stink of mould. His cadaverous face was mottled and white; his eyes, no longer dark, shone like polished steel. He gazed at her and Hallkell, angry but puzzled, as if unsure what to do next. Svana felt faint; Agmundr didn't recognise her. But then he lifted one side of his mouth. At the sight of his gentle, familiar smile, Svana wept and laughed as tears spilled on her cheeks.

"Agmundr," she said, letting go of the knife. "My love, you've come back."

With a roar, Hallkell punched Agmundr clear across the room. Agmundr crashed into the wall like a cannonball, the force bowing and splintering the wood panels. His head and spine must surely be broken. Svana hugged herself tightly.

The fight was over.

But no, unfazed, Agmundr pushed himself clear and landed on his feet.

Svana put her hands to her mouth. This wasn't Agmundr anymore, she reminded herself, giddy with shock and revulsion, but a supernatural being.

The Again-Walkers circled each other. They stood between her and the door. Svana held the apron of her overdress to her nose. The stench of rotting flesh made her gag. She tore the blind from the largest window. Could she fit? Yes, she would be able to wriggle her shoulders through well enough, but what about her hips? The risk of getting stuck was too great. Reaching the door was her only chance.

Head down, Hallkell rushed and caught Agmundr. The momentum of the charge rammed Agmundr into the kitchen shelves. Shards of wood and broken ceramics exploded across the kitchen. Svana bolted for the door, her shoes crunching over debris. Something sharp opened her foot. She cried out and fell.

Hallkell slammed his massive shoulder into Agmundr once more. The wall behind them caved. Surely, neighbours must hear the commotion. But who would dare investigate? And with her foot split from toe to heel, running away would now be impossible. What should she do? Try to hide while the battle raged around her, praying to the gods that she wouldn't be crushed?

Agmundr grabbed the iron pot from the fire and struck Hallkell across the face. There was an audible crack. Boiling water and vegetables sprayed in an arc. Hallkell lost his grip and sprawled onto his back. When he gathered his limbs beneath him to stand up, Svana saw that the blow had sheared the skin from his cheekbone as neatly as if dissected by a filleting knife. Agmundr struck again with the pot. A dozen of Hallkell's yellow teeth spilled across the floor.

Of course, the supernatural power of iron...

To kill an Again-Walker, you must cut off its head with an iron sword.

Svana remembered the marital sword hanging on the wall, the iron sword that had held their wedding rings, and crawled towards it. Her injured foot left a long, wide trail of blood. She must have severed an artery. One way or another, she would die this night. Damn her brother. If he had held his temper, none of these terrible events would have happened.

The feud between the Jenson and Norup families had started because of cabbage seeds. At great expense, her brother had purchased 10,000 seeds from Hallkell's father and had sown an entire field. The seeds had rotted in the dirt. They had been too old to germinate. Hallkell's father had refused to repay the purchase price, let alone give compensation for the loss of income a failed acre would cause. The farm had only been three acres in total, with one acre already lying fallow to rest the soil. Enraged, her brother had killed him with a rock to the temple.

Hatred for her brother burned in Svana's belly and gave her strength. Crawling faster, she stayed along the walls, giving the Again-Walkers a wide berth.

Hallkell punched Agmundr across the room and fell upon him, pummelling with both fists, again and again, until Svana was sure that Agmundr must be in pieces.

Groping his hand along the floor, Agmundr found the knife she had dropped. With a shout, he thrust the iron blade into Hallkell's eye. Hallkell howled, staggered away, pulled out the knife and threw it aside. Agmundr leapt up, grabbed a chair and broke it over him; grabbed the table and broke that over him too. Hallkell swept an arm and slammed Agmundr to the ground. In a trice, Agmundr leapt up and attacked again. Neither of them seemed fatigued or bothered by injury, as if they could keep assailing each other until the end of the world, until Ragnarok.

Svana got to her feet, lunged for the sword, and pulled it from its bracket.

Nearly a metre long, the sword was heavy.

She staggered beneath its weight, her muscles straining and pulling. The hilt was wrapped in leather thong, the blade decorated with a herringbone pattern-weld. How fitting: Hallkell had made the very sword that would send him to the afterlife. With difficulty, she slung the sword over one shoulder.

"Agmundr," she cried. "Look out."

Clenching her teeth with effort, she swung the sword double-handed into Hallkell's neck. Sparking and smoking with an unknown alchemy, the iron blade sliced through the thick and sinewy throat as if through a bowl of soft curds. The head fell away. Svana dropped the sword. A blustery, sighing exhalation issued from the severed neck. Hallkell's remaining eye glittered once and went out.

"Is it over?" Svana said. "Is he finally dead?"

Agmundr did not reply. Together, they stared at Hallkell.

A ghostly blue mist rose from the body, curling like steam. The mist began to glisten with thousands of lights, each one as tiny as a dust mote. Hallkell's corpse rippled and wrinkled as if countless mice were running beneath his skin. Horrified, Svana could not look away. The blue mist flared and crackled. With a stink of ozone, the mist erupted into an intense bright light that shone through her eyelids. She flung an arm over her face and screamed. The light went out as suddenly as it had appeared.

Hesitantly, Svana dared to look.

The mist had cleared.

The colossal and blackened Again-Walker was gone. In its place lay Hallkell, human and dead for three days, waxy, streaming with putrefaction juices.

Praise Odin.

Exhausted, Svana collapsed. A puddle of blood surrounded her injured foot. She would have to staunch the bleeding, and quick.

Already, she felt her strength waning and her vision fading.

Agmundr sat on the floor nearby. The awful marbling of his chalk-white face made her whimper. He smiled at her with one side of his mouth and reached out his hand, as if to say, *come to me, don't be afraid*. And what did she have to fear? His love for her was so great that he had defied death in order to save her from Hallkell.

Relief gave her the shivers. Beginning to sob, she crawled over.

Dagny's remains lay at the door. Stupid old woman, Svana thought. Not all men are as selfish as you would have had me believe.

Drained, Svana reached out to her lover.

Agmundr took her in his arms and held her tightly.

Her terror ebbed away. His body felt as cold and dense as clay, but it did not matter. She would get used to his physical changes; would come to adore his eerie, mirrored eyes, learn to put up with his dank smell. He hadn't spoken a single word this whole time. Had he lost the power of speech? Well, that did not matter either.

Safe, she relaxed against Agmundr's chest.

"Ours is a true love," she said at last. "Not even death can separate us."

He took her by the shoulders and held her at arm's length.

Svana opened her eyes, already smiling with gratitude and devotion. His smile, in return, was pitiless. Svana's heart began to thud. She tried to pull away but the grip on her was impossibly strong. Fingers dug into her flesh. Yes, she would die this very night, but not from the severed artery in her foot.

"Please," she whispered. "Please don't."

The Again-Walker's mouldering lips drew back to show long fangs.

And then it set upon her.

END

BIOGRAPHY

DEBORAH SHELDON is an award-winning author from Melbourne, Australia, who writes short stories, novellas and novels across the darker spectrum of horror, crime and noir. Her award-nominated titles include the novels *Body Farm Z*, *Contrition* and *Devil Dragon*; the novella *Thylacines*; and collection *Figments and Fragments: Dark Stories*. Her collection *Perfect Little Stitches and Other Stories* won the Australian Shadows 'Best Collected Work' Award, was shortlisted for an Aurealis Award, and long-listed for a Bram Stoker. She has won the Australian Shadows 'Best Edited Work' Award twice; as editor of *Midnight Echo 14*, and for the anthology she conceived and edited *Spawn: Weird Horror Tales About Pregnancy, Birth and Babies*. Deb's short fiction has appeared in many well-respected magazines such as *Quadrant*, *Island*, *Aurealis*, *Midnight Echo*, *Andromeda Spaceways, AntipodeanSF* and *Dimension6*, been nominated for various awards, and included in 'best of' anthologies including *Year's Best Hardcore Horror*. Her previous titles with Demain Publishing are *Hand to Mouth* and *Garland Cove*. Other credits include feature articles for Australian and international magazines, non-fiction books

(Reed Books, Random House), TV scripts such as NEIGHBOURS, stage plays, and award-winning medical writing.

Visit Deborah at:
http://deborahsheldon.wordpress.com

ADRIAN BALDWIN (COVER ARTIST)

Adrian is a Mancunian now living and working in Wales. Back in the 1990s, he wrote for various TV shows/personalities: Smith & Jones, Clive Anderson, Brian Conley, Paul McKenna, Hale & Pace, Rory Bremner (and a few others). Wooo, get him! Since then, he has written three screenplays—one of which received generous financial backing from the Film Agency for Wales. Then along came the global recession which kicked the UK Film industry in the nuts. What a bummer! Not to be outdone, he turned to novel writing—which had always been his real dream—and, in particular, a genre he feels is often overlooked; a genre he has always been a fan of: Dark Comedy (sometimes referred to as Horror's weird cousin). *Barnacle Brat* (a dark comedy for grown-ups), his first novel won Indie Novel of the Year 2016 award; his second novel *Stanley Mccloud Must Die!* (more dark comedy for grown-ups) published in 2016 and his third: *The Snowman And The Scarecrow* (another dark comedy for grown-ups) published in 2018. Adrian Baldwin has also written and published a number of dark comedy short stories. He designs book covers too—not just for his own books but for a growing number of publishers.

For more information on the award-winning author, check out:

https://adrianbaldwin.info/

DEMAIN PUBLISHING

To keep up to-date on all news DEMAIN (including future submission calls and releases) you can follow us in a number of ways:

BLOG:
www.demainpublishingblog.weebly.com

TWITTER:
@DemainPubUk

FACEBOOK PAGE:
Demain Publishing

INSTAGRAM:
demainpublishing

www.ingramcontent.com/pod-product-compliance
Lightning Source LLC
LaVergne TN
LVHW041132150826
845673LV00007B/2292

9798846086906